BUS RHYME
AND PLAYTIME

For the bus enthusiast

Bus, bus, bus, bus, bussy, bussy, bus, bus.

Award-winning author – 'The Wishing Shelf Book Awards'

Published in 2023 by JayJayBooks
ISBN: 978-1-9163923-5-9

Written by Sue Wickstead
Illustrations by Artful Doodlers
Layout design by Claire Shaw

BUS RHYMES
AND PLAYTIME

SUE WICKSTEAD

To Mandy and Maggie, in Ipswich,
who like to share bus rhymes with little visitors.

And in memory of Ian from Hackney
who taught me to 'Zoom to the Moon'.

For Alexander who helped to sing the songs.

CONTENTS

Tickets please!

Stick, stick, stick, stick, sticky, sticky, stick, stick.

THE BUS RIDE

We're going on a bus ride.
Hooray! Hooray!
Where will we go?
Will it take all day?

We've got our tickets ready.
We're waiting at the stop.
Along comes the bus,
And onto it we hop.

Child Single

Have you
ever been
on a
bus ride?

FIVE LITTLE BUSES

Five little buses went driving one day,
Over the hills and far away.
Along the road, and down the track,
but... one got stuck in a traffic jam.
So only four little buses came back.

Four little buses went driving one day,

Over the hills and far away.

Along the road and down the track,

but... one got stuck in a narrow lane.

So only three little buses came back.

Three little buses went driving one day,

Over the hills and far away.

Along the road and down the track,

but... one got stuck under a bridge.

So only two little buses came back.

Two little buses went driving one day,
Over the hills and far away.
Along the road and down the track,
but... one got stuck up a steep hill!
So only one little bus came back.

One little bus went driving one day,
Over the hills and far away.
Along the road and down the track,
but... what's that noise? Beep, beep, beep!
Hooray! All five little buses came back.

Beep, beep, beep, beep, beep!

Child Return

Where would
you like
to go on a
bus ride?

DAVID'S BATH TIME ADVENTURE

Time for your bath,
Says David's mum.
With bubbles and buses
He has lots of fun.

For David

Splash, splash, splash, splash,
splashy, splashy, splash, splash.

ALL DAY LONG

Daisy's wheels go round and round,
round and round, round and round.
Daisy's wheels go round and round,
All day long.
(Where will she visit today?)

Jay-Jay's horn goes beep, beep, beep,
Beep, beep, beep. Beep, beep, beep.
Jay-Jay's horn goes beep, beep, beep,
All day long.
(Can you hear him?)

Gloria's doors, they open and shut,
Open and shut, open and shut.
Gloria's doors, they open and shut,
All day long.
(They make a pshh pshh sound.)

Real Bus Rhyme Time

Head to page 28 for
the Real Bus Rhyme Time

Sparky's driver says, "Come on board,
Come on board, come on board.
Sparky's driver says, "Come on board,"
All day long.
(Will you join in the fun?)

BARTY'S THOUGHTS

There are lots and lots of teddy bears,
A little worse for wear,
It doesn't mean they should be thrown,
They just need a little care.

All our childhood memories
Should not be thrown away,
They hold some special stories,
Of when we used to play.

Of times when we were lonely,
Feeling poorly, scared or sad,
A squeeze from your teddy bear
And you wouldn't feel so bad.

Our bears so full of cuddles.
Would guard you day and night.
They'd listen to your worries
And make you feel all right.

Teddy bears, floppy dogs,
Any soft toy would do.
Barty was a special bear,
Do you have one too?

 What toy would you take on a bus ride?

Child — Return — 8:43am

17

JAY-JAY'S ISLAND ADVENTURE

Jay-Jay is off to an island.
He's got to go by ferry.
He drives on very quickly.
He's feeling very merry.

Jay-Jay has bumped his bottom.
He is feeling very sad.
They fix it with some plaster.
It doesn't look that bad.

A special Playbus visit,
Filled with toys and books.
Children run excitedly.
They want to take a look.

At the end of the adventure,
Which has been lots of fun.
It's time to board the boat again,
But this time, he won't run.

Child Return

Have you
ever seen a bus
on a ferry?

Child Single

Have you ever
been on a boat?

DAVID'S BIN DAY

David's Wednesday is full of fun,
That's the day when the bin men come.
He puts a bobble hat on his head,
Just like them he's a bin man instead.

He hears the truck coming up the street
And sees the men with their marching feet.
Black sacks in bins are loaded on,
And with a crunch the rubbish is gone.

On which day does your bin man come?

icket ticket ticket ticket ticket ticket ticket ticket ticket ticket ticket ticket

Adult Return

That's a game David wants to play,
He finds some things to throw away.
Any small toys left on the floor,
Go into his bin then he looks for more.

With a noisy grumble and a bump
From behind the sofa and into the dump.
It's a tidy house on bin men day.
But, where have your things gone today?

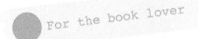

For the book lover

Book, book, book, book, booky,
booky, book, book.

21

THE SPOOKY BUS RIDE

Nanny, Nanny!

There's a witch on the bus
And she's casting lots of spells.
She's stirring up her cooking pot,
And making lots of smells!
(Pooey!)

Nanny, Nanny!

There's a dinosaur on the bus.
He's taking up all the room.
The witch is shooing him away
With her big and bristly broom.
(Whack!)

Nanny, Nanny!

There's a bear on the bus.
He's looking very mad.
I think he's a lost teddy bear,
Which is making him feel sad.
(I'll give him a cuddle. Aww!)

Nanny, Nanny!

There's a gorilla on the bus,
And he's been beating on his chest.
It's made him feel quite tired,
So now he needs a rest.
(Shh! Don't wake him.)

23

Nanny, Nanny!

There's a dragon on the bus.
He's puffing out black smoke.
He sat down very quickly,
When the witch firmly spoke.
(Good dragon.)

Nanny, Nanny!

There are monsters on the bus.
What on earth shall we do?
"Just come and sit down quietly,
The only monster here is you."
(Not really.)

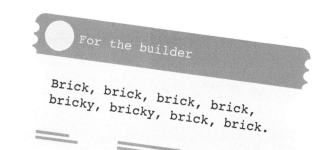

For the builder

Brick, brick, brick, brick,
bricky, bricky, brick, brick.

THREE LITTLE MEN IN A FLYING SAUCER

Three little men in a flying saucer,
Flew round the world one day.
They looked left and right,
But they didn't like the sight,
So one man flew away.

Two little men in a flying saucer,
Flew round the world one day.
They looked left and right,
But they didn't like the sight,
So, one man flew away.

One little man in a flying saucer,
Flew round the world one day.
He looked down at us,
And he saw our bus,
So he said, "I think I'll stay."

DRIVE, DRIVE, DRIVE THE BUS

Drive, drive, drive the bus
Slowly down the lane.
Did you catch the big red bus?
Aren't you glad you came?

Drive, drive, drive the bus
Slowly down the lane.
Did you have a ticket?
Will you come again?

REAL BUS RHYME TIME

Daisy's wheels go round and round

Jay-Jay's horn goes beep, beep, beep

Gloria's doors, they open and shut

Sparky's driver says, "Come on board"

Books by Sue Wickstead

Award-winning author – 'The Wishing Shelf Book Awards'
Sue Wickstead is an author and Primary School teacher working across Sussex and Surrey. For over twenty years, alongside her teaching career, she has worked with a children's charity, The Bewbush Playbus Association, which inspired the Jay-Jay series of books.
www.suewickstead.co.uk

Milton Keynes UK
Ingram Content Group UK Ltd.
UKHW050011080324
439015UK00004B/27